Maitland's Kid

by
Anne Schraff

Perfection Learning Corporation
Logan, Iowa 51546

Cover: Doug Knutson

1 A BRIGHT SUN lit the narrow road before Jonathan's old VW bus. The boy's hands tensed on the wheel. Blue veins popped up from under his skin. He wasn't exactly sure why he was doing this after all these years.

"I'm going to see my dad," Jonathan had told his mother yesterday, as they sat in their big home in Heritage Hills.

Jonathan had thought of going to see his father many times. But now, at last, he was actually doing it. So why now?

It had been a lousy year for him. He hadn't made any of the varsity teams. And once again the counselor had said he was "poorly adjusted, unsocial, a loner."

Those disappointments weighed on him until the dream of going to Stony River finally became a plan. Now, more than ever before, Jonathan needed something from his father.

He'd tried to explain that to his mother. "Maybe my dad will understand me," he'd said.

She'd smiled bitterly. "He's known

where you lived for sixteen years, Jon. He's never even written. I'm surprised you'd look for understanding from a stranger."

But, on this first day of Christmas vacation, Jonathan had packed a suitcase and started west.

It was only a hundred miles to the country town where Ed Maitland lived. When Jonathan was younger, he'd wondered why his dad never made the trip.

At first he had invented crazy excuses to explain it. He imagined his father was a secret agent for the government. Or that he was the captain of a cruise ship that only docked in Europe.

Sometimes Jonathan dreamed of the fantastic reunion he and his father would share. One day his dad would be at the door, his arms wide open.

As Jonathan got older, he thought his father might be afraid to show himself. But now he figured his dad knew he didn't belong in Heritage Hills—not any more than Jonathan did.

Jonathan slowed as he entered Stony River. The little drugstore featured what must have been one of the last soda fountains in the country. And in the hardware store, hand-lettered signs trumpeted feed and grain specials.

Jonathan glanced nervously from side to side. He didn't know exactly where his father lived. His only address was a post office box. To that address Jonathan's mother sent brief reports of Jonathan's progress. And from that address came no reply.

Jonathan pulled in front of the hardware store. Beside the doorway sat two old men enjoying the winter sun. They looked like they would know where every last soul in Stony River lived.

"Hi," Jonathan called.

They didn't answer right away. They narrowed their eyes to squints and stared at Jonathan. Their glance wasn't friendly, and Jonathan felt out of place. After all, he wasn't dressed like the local boys. His hands were smooth, not calloused. And Stony River probably didn't like the loud music that blared from his VW.

"Whyn't you turn down that racket?" one of the men suggested, spitting a stream of tobacco juice at a tree.

"Oh, you mean my radio?"

"Don't mean the birds," the man snapped in a voice as crisp as the frosty air.

Jonathan wondered if his father was like this, a narrow man with squinty eyes. Still, his dad would be younger. He'd only be thirty-eight. But in all other respects, he might be like these men. Maybe everybody in Stony River was like them.

Jonathan switched off the radio. Then he turned back to ask, "Could you tell me where Ed Maitland lives?"

"Who're you?" asked the old man in the railroad cap.

"I'm Jonathan Grant." He never used his father's name. His stepfather, Barry Grant, had adopted Jonathan as a baby. Barry was the closest thing to a father he'd ever had.

"Don't mean a thing to me," said the tobacco chewer. He crossed his rangy legs and spit again.

"Look, I'm his son. I'm Maitland's kid."

The squinty eyes blinked. "Well, that's a real news flash!"

"Could you just tell me where he lives?" Jonathan asked.

Perhaps he'd spoken too sharply, for the two men instantly rose and walked toward the door of the hardware store.

"Boy, you guys aren't real polite, are you?" Jonathan shouted after them.

The man in the railroad cap stopped and turned around. "Young folks 'round here don't just come up to their elders and demand to know everybody's business. You ain't from around here. That's clear as December ice. Whyn't you just jump in that noisy car of yours and go back to the city, boy?" With that the old man stalked off.

Shaking his head, Jonathan turned and studied the main street to look for another likely source of information. What a one-horse town it was! Barry, his stepfather, would laugh at such a place—

and those two old men. "Jerkwater Joe's," he would call them.

Barry was very smooth and glib. He was the kind of guy with a million friends. Jonathan used to admire Barry. In fact, for the most part, he still did. After all, Barry was witty and cool and an all-American college football player. His name was always in the paper for "civic honors and achievements."

There was a time Jonathan wanted to be exactly like Barry. But then, little by little, he saw he never could be.

Suddenly Jonathan realized there was a girl standing by his side. Jonathan stared at her reddish hair, which glittered like copper wire in the sun.

"Hi. You look sorta lost," she said.

Jonathan smiled, grateful for a friendly face. "I am, in a way."

"I'm Liz Finch," she said. "My folks run the coffee shop and cabins across the street."

"I'm Jonathan Grant. I came here to see my real dad. His name's Ed Maitland. I bet you know him."

She shrugged and her friendly smile faded a little. "He never mentioned a son."

"I was adopted by my mom's second husband when I was a baby. I've never seen my father, but I'd like to meet him now. Can you tell me where he lives?"

"Come on over to the coffee shop."

As they crossed the street, Jonathan spotted a man changing a tire in the gas station in front of the coffee shop. He was about forty years old and had thinning red hair.

Jonathan stared at him, wondering if this was his father. Could his dad be this skinny guy with a long nose and small blue eyes creased with laugh lines?

Jonathan felt numb, wondering what he'd say. As many times as he'd imagined their reunion, he'd never really planned that out.

Then Liz said, "Hey, Pop, listen to this." She repeated what Jonathan had told her.

Mr. Finch examined Jonathan. "You don't favor him, looks-wise," he finally said. He wiped the grease off his hands with an old rag and continued. "Well, supposing I tell Maitland you're here. My wife'll fix you something to eat while you wait. If he wants to come talk to you, he can."

"Look!" Jonathan shouted. He was getting angry. "What's with this town? This is still the United States of America, right? A free country and all that. What's the matter with just giving me my father's address?"

Mr. Finch softly cut in. "Not up to me to invade a neighbor's privacy. Folks in Stony River respect such things. Maybe Maitland don't want a stranger beating a path to his door."

"I'm his *son*."

"You told Liz you've never seen him. That makes you a stranger."

Jonathan thought it over and then nodded. He didn't have much choice.

Reluctantly, he followed Liz into the coffee shop. There she introduced him to her mother, who quickly brought Jonathan a tasty bowl of chili with crackers.

As he ate, Liz took up the conversation again. "Didn't you write him and say you were coming or anything?" she asked.

"No."

"That's weird. You could scare the daylights out of him."

"I didn't plan on coming until the last minute. I just packed a suitcase and jumped in the car. Actually, I've been thinking about doing it all my life. Every other time, I chickened out."

Liz shook her head. "I'd be scared to just pop in on somebody and say, 'Hi, I'm your kid.' "

"Liz, do you know my father? I mean, what's he like?"

"Didn't your mom tell you about him?" Liz asked.

"Yeah, a little. They got married real young. He was in the Army. Mom came from a better family, kind of . . . and I guess everything went sour real fast. I never knew him. I have a picture of him though."

Jonathan fished out the cracked, old snapshot of the gaunt GI from his pocket.

"Here . . . does he look much like that anymore? I guess not, huh?"

Liz looked at the picture and shook her head.

"Well, what's he do . . . I mean, for a living, you know?" Jonathan eagerly asked.

Liz nibbled on a cracker. "This and that."

"What's the big secret?"

"Oh, it's not that. It's just . . . around here, we don't talk behind folks' backs."

"Can you at least tell me if you like him?"

Liz smiled. "Yeah. We all do." She paused and then asked. "You've told me family history, but what about *you*?"

Jonathan cradled a cup of coffee in his hands and told Liz about himself. "I'm kind of a square peg in a round hole. My half brother and half sister, they couldn't be more like my parents . . . I mean Mom and Barry, my stepfather. They're all real social and great athletes.

"But me, I've always been called a loner. People don't take to me very well.

"I feel weird being so different. I thought if I met my real dad, maybe he'd understand and help me to understand. Do you know what I mean?"

Liz laughed. She had a noisy, open-throated laugh that reminded Jonathan of his plump Aunt Suzy. But Liz was slim as a pencil.

"Maybe you're just an original, Jonathan."

"Oddball is more the word. I feel like Jeff and Gigi—my half brother and sister—belong in the Grant family. They belong in Heritage Hills. But I don't."

Liz smiled again. She was pretty in the way wildflowers are—loose and straggly in places, but adding up nicely. Gigi was a city flower. Every petal was perfect.

"I guess everybody feels like that sometimes, Jonathan," she said.

Jonathan glanced up at the clock and saw that Mr. Finch had been gone for forty minutes. Where was he? Jonathan's stomach started to ache.

Then he heard a car pull up outside. Jonathan's hands tightened. A volcano churned inside him. All these years of wondering. Now, in a second or two, his father would be coming through that broken screen door.

Liz got up and moved towards the kitchen to give Jonathan privacy. "I hope it's nice for you, Jonathan," she said.

"Yeah, thanks," Jonathan replied in a cracked voice.

The door opened. Mr. Finch was alone. He pulled off his heavy jacket and turned to Jonathan. "I'm sorry. He didn't want to come."

Jonathan felt like somebody had punched his aching stomach. Anxiety flowed out and anger flowed in.

"I don't believe it! I mean, he can't know I've come all this way to see him and then just . . . just not want to see me!"

"I'm sorry," Mr. Finch said again.

"Look, if I could just see him and . . . "

"He doesn't want to see you. That's how it is, boy. I'm really very sorry, but there's nothing I can do."

2 FOR A MOMENT, Jonathan sat there coldly, feeling like he was lost at sea.

"Look," Mr. Finch said, "it's getting late. Why don't you spend the night with us? You can get an early start in the morning."

The anger inside the boy exploded. "No! I'm not going home until I've seen my father!" He got up, almost knocking his chair backwards. "You won't tell me where he is, huh?"

Mr. Finch looked down at the flowered oilcloth on the table. He didn't say a word.

Jonathan put down the money for the chili and coffee, then strode outside. It was a lot colder now than it had been when he first came. Clouds were building, looking like dirty snowbanks. Jonathan stuck his red, stiff hands into his pockets and looked up and down the darkening street.

Where was he? Where was his father hiding? Was he skulking behind the counter of the drugstore? Maybe he was breaking off flakes of hay at some run-down farm. Maybe he was sitting in the corner of that dark bar where blue and red neon gases kept blinking out "Beer & Wine" against the darkening sky.

Jonathan moved grimly to his VW. Maybe his mom was right. Maybe Ed Maitland was just no good.

Jonathan lay awake in the back of the bus for a long time. He tried to put together the bits and pieces his mother had given him about his father. Jonathan remembered her using words like "immature" and "irresponsible." She acted as if the marriage had been a total mistake—as if she wished Barry had been her first and only husband.

But things weren't that tidy. She had Jonathan as a reminder of her mistake. And although nobody ever came out and said it, he didn't seem to have his life together like his brother and sister.

Sometimes Jonathan wondered if that was because he was Maitland's kid and they were Barry's kids. If Maitland was no good, then maybe Jonathan was just fruit from a bad tree.

Maybe Jonathan was selfish like him, too. Maybe even making this trip was a selfish thing to do.

* * *

Jonathan was up with the sun. Sleep had given him a new energy and fixed purpose. He was now determined to find his father by any means available.

After eating breakfast from the food supplies in his VW, Jonathan stopped at the hardware store. He bought a sack of grain and then drove west.

He stopped at the first farm he saw. "Hi," he called out, startling the teenager who was fixing a fence. "I'm supposed to deliver this grain to Ed Maitland. Know where his place is? I'm new around here."

The farm kid grinned, a big wide gum grin.

"You pullin' my leg?" he chuckled.

"No, I gotta deliver this grain and . . . "

"Who on earth are you?" the boy asked, still grinning.

"I was told Maitland's farm was around here," Jonathan said.

"Aw, shoot. Somebody's pullin' your leg!" The boy slapped his thigh and laughed.

Jonathan roared off, digging ruts in the road with his tires. He returned to town and pulled up to the bar. It wasn't open yet, but a man was mopping inside. He turned when Jonathan rapped on the window.

"Hey, mister. Can I talk to you a minute?"

"We're open at two," the man shouted.

"No, I just want to talk."

The man came closer. An unsightly burn scar dominated one side of his face. His hair was disheveled and badly in need of a washing.

"This place opens at two. That's all I know," he called as he walked off, pushing the mop before him.

Jonathan turned away in disgust. But his eyes lightened when he saw some kids playing in the back of a pickup truck. Maybe they'd know where Ed Maitland lived or worked.

"Hi," Jonathan said. "I'm new in town.

I'm looking . . . "

"Hey!" A sharp voice came from behind Jonathan. "Whatcha want with my kids?" Jonathan turned and found the speaker was a dark-bearded man of about forty.

"I was just asking directions," Jonathan explained. This angry man could be Ed Maitland. The thin face in the faded picture could have aged into this angry bearded face.

But then the scarred face of the mop man could equally have belonged to his father. In fact, his father could be any middle-aged male in this scary town.

"Don't mess with my kids, stranger," snarled the man.

Jonathan hurried away. He climbed into his VW and thought about heading home. But, before he did that, he intended to stop at Finch's coffee shop and tell them what he thought of this crummy town.

He found Mr. Finch and Liz inside the garage, working together on the engine of an old sedan. Liz wore an old scarf

around her head. Her clothes, hands—
even her face—were smeared with grease.

Jonathan had never seen a girl looking
so messy. He tried to imagine any girl at
Heritage Hills High in a similar situation.
He couldn't.

Jonathan walked up to them and an-
nounced, "You people will be happy to
know I'm leaving. But before I go, I just
wanted to tell you what I think of Stony
River. All I wanted was to see my dad,
but everyone here has treated me like a
criminal or something." Jonathan's voice
was shaking.

Mr. Finch sighed. "Don't you think we
should respect a man's wishes about who
he wants to see?"

"I've got a right to see my dad!"
Jonathan almost shouted. Even as his
own words rang in the air, he again heard
his counselor's words: "immature, poor
control of his temper."

"Well," Mr. Finch sighed again, "tell
you what. I won't say where he lives, but
I'll do this much for you. Around noon
he usually comes in here to have lunch.

You can see him then.

"But don't tell him I pointed him out. I'm asking that of you 'cause I don't want to lose his friendship."

Jonathan was astonished; the man was giving in! His hands began to shake, and he mumbled thanks to Mr. Finch as he exited the garage.

Outside, he walked into the middle of a snow flurry. The big wet flakes quickly covered everything. But it was too warm for the snow to last. Rain soon followed and drowned the snow's beauty.

For a moment, Jonathan felt sorry for the snowflakes melting before the downpour. Then he caught himself. Feeling sorry for snowflakes! Who else would have such a dumb idea?

A little before noon, Jonathan hurried into the coffee shop. He took a corner table and sipped hot coffee, glancing nervously at each customer.

A fat man with a shiny bald head sat at a nearby table with a woman. As he spoke to the woman, the man frequently laughed.

Would he be laughing like that if he'd just sent away his poor wretch of a son? Jonathan didn't think so.

A handsome man in a white shirt was having a hamburger alone. He had deep, sad eyes. Jonathan's heart quickened. The guy looked a little like the Army youth in the faded picture. He was good-looking and dignified. Jonathan stared at him; his mouth went dry. That must be his real father!

Suddenly the door opened and the mop man came in. He took a booth near the window.

Liz appeared at Jonathan's side. "By the window," she whispered.

Jonathan's heart lurched. The disfigured man. The shabby, broken-down mop man. Jonathan gulped his coffee and snatched a few quick glimpses. He felt no part of this dirty stranger. Shouldn't he feel *something* for him?

But the only thing he felt right now was his skin crawling. In fact, Jonathan was sorry he'd ever come to Stony River. He just wanted to finish his coffee in one great gulp and run to his VW, breaking all speed records to get home.

Yet Jonathan couldn't. It was as though the mop man held a key, a key that would explain why Jonathan's own life seemed to be going wrong.

Jonathan forced himself to get up and go over to the window booth. In a hollow, high-pitched kid's voice he squawked, "Are you Ed Maitland?"

The man didn't look up right away. He took a final swallow of coffee with a strange kind of doomed resignation. He seemed to be bracing himself. Then his gaze jerked up and he said, "Finch said you were in town. And I told him I didn't want to see you." His voice was flat and emotionless.

"I just want a couple a minutes . . . Dad," Jonathan forced the word out. He was surprised he could even bring himself to use the word.

"Don't call me Dad. Barry Grant is your dad," Ed Maitland retorted.

"Can I sit down for a minute?" Jonathan asked. His mind was spinning like a kid's top. For a crazy moment he thought he was dreaming or maybe having a nightmare.

"I've got nothing to say to you." With that, Maitland got up, put on his overcoat and cap, and walked silently out of the coffee shop.

Jonathan hesitated, then followed like a mangy pup dogging an indifferent stranger.

"Hey, listen, I came a long way to see you," he protested when he caught up with Ed Maitland. He knew he was whining. He didn't want to, but he was.

"I didn't ask you to come," Maitland said, staring straight ahead.

"You so busy you can't spare me a couple of minutes?" The whining little-boy voice shrieked out from all those years he'd spent wondering about this man.

"I gotta clean up another store before I quit."

"How about after? Could I come to your place?"

Maitland stopped walking and turned to face Jonathan. "No!" he shouted. "Go home. Go back where you belong."

For the first time, Jonathan really looked at the man. He noticed Maitland had light blue eyes, like Jonathan's.

Everybody else in the Grant family had brown eyes. Nobody had ever told Jonathan that his father had light blue eyes. And you couldn't tell from the black and white snapshot.

Jonathan looked closer and saw a lot of himself in the damaged, angry face before him. The high cheekbones, the gauntness—that was what Jonathan saw when he looked in the mirror.

A lump rose in Jonathan's throat and crazy tears threatened behind his eyes.

"I want just a few minutes to talk. Please."

"I've nothing to say to you. Nothing worth you hearing. I'm a bum. I'm a wino who does what he has to do to stay alive. You're doing fine. Your mother tells me now and then how well you're doing, grades and all. Be satisfied with that and leave me alone, can't you?"

"I'm not doing fine!" Jonathan said.

"Get outta my sight." The man shouted with such fury that Jonathan thought he might lash out. "Y'hear me? Get away from me."

In stunned silence, Jonathan stood and watched the man move off and disappear into the drugstore. Numbness crept over him, and then he felt wet drops on his cheeks. He dragged his sleeve across his face with such angry force that he cut his cheek on a cuff button.

"Jonathan?" Liz asked behind him. "Why don't you come back in the shop for another cup of coffee?"

Too drained to protest, Jonathan nodded and followed. Inside he found the other customers were gone.

He sat quietly for a few minutes across from Liz. Finally he blurted out, "He's a jerk."

"I'm sorry it had to be that way for you."

"You've known him all your life, huh, Liz?"

"Yeah."

"Funny, you know him and I don't.

And I'm his kid."

Liz shrugged and said nothing.

"He's a janitor, right?" Jonathan asked. He pondered the idea of a man, nearly forty years old, living his life behind a mop. "Well, I'm sorry I came, that's for sure."

"You know, like they say, it's sometimes better to let sleeping dogs lie."

"I bet he lives in some shack, huh?"

"Yes," Liz said.

"Just a bum. Nothing special, I guess. I suppose he isn't into saving the wilderness or anything?"

"Don't try to label him, Jonathan. Everybody is special in their own way," Liz said.

"It's funny," Jonathan said bitterly, "for a little while I thought he'd be like that guy, Thoreau. You know, that writer who lived in the woods trying to find the real meaning of life."

"He never talked about Thoreau that I remember. He might've said something about writing."

"Does he drink a lot? He said he was

a wino."

"I expect we shouldn't judge, Jonathan."

"Boy, how about this for a memory? A guy comes a hundred miles for *this*. My folks said not to come. As usual, they were right and I was wrong."

Liz stirred her coffee silently. In his heart, Jonathan knew she was acting a lot more mature than he was. But if Maitland were her father . . .

"Well, that's about it then . . . nothing left to say," Jonathan said. "Nothing good about him."

"He treats everybody right, Jonathan," she protested.

"What's that mean?"

"He's a friend if you need one—and a good neighbor. He never bothers anybody. Minds his own business. Maybe that's enough." Liz looked Jonathan right in the eye.

"Well, he makes me sick, I'll tell you that, Liz. This whole town makes me sick. I'm going home."

"That's probably best, Jonathan."

"Yeah."

They said goodbye and Jonathan went outside. He found his VW and got in. He smiled bitterly as he thought about all the long talks he'd planned to have with his father when they finally met. He had intended to trot out all his problems, hoping that good old dad could help. What a load of nonsense that turned out to be! What a load of childish nonsense.

Jonathan trembled with frustration and anger. He glared at the thick, black clouds that were full of snow and wind. Then he started the engine.

As he sped down the street, Jonathan grieved that now when he thought of Ed Maitland, there wouldn't be a shred of mystery left. No doubt. And no warmth. It was better before. Not knowing was better than this.

Jonathan was heading out of town when he saw the solitary figure moving down the side of the highway. He was hunched over as before, but this time he was unsteady, too. Obviously he had already been to the bar.

Maitland ambled off the highway toward a cabin set back among the trees. It was a sloppy-looking bum's roost.

Jonathan looked away. He didn't need this. Not this final, awful sight to remember his father by. It was a dirty trick of fate.

And then Maitland stumbled on a patch of ice. Jonathan had looked again, even though he didn't want to. Sometimes you watch things because you have to, even though they rip you apart inside.

Maitland tried to get up. He put the palms of his hands on the ice and started to stand. But his legs skidded out from under him. He looked like a bad clown in a cheap circus show. Once, twice more, and then he stopped trying.

Cursing, Jonathan pulled the VW over and halted. He had to help Maitland into his cabin or the man would freeze to death.

Jonathan reached a hand out to his father. "Here, let me help you."

"Blast it," Maitland gasped in a

whisky-slurred voice. "Can't you leave me alone?"

3 JONATHAN DROPPED HIS hand and stepped back. He had never seen a man so spit-fire angry. Maitland tried to get up again but stumbled and cursed at himself. Once more Jonathan held out his hand.

This time his father finally accepted his help. But even as he did so, he growled, "Damn."

Jonathan got him through the unlocked door and into the dark, cold cabin.

"Man!" Jonathan complained, "it's freezing in here!" The boy hugged himself and did a little jig to keep warm. He looked around, taking in the shambles of his father's dwelling. An old cot, a broken chair, a stove, an icebox, and cartons filled with junk. That was it. There was a fireplace, but nothing was in it but cold ashes.

"Where do you keep your firewood?" Jonathan asked.

Maitland sat on his cot with his head down. His thick, black hair, streaked with grey, hung in his face. "Get out," he said softly.

"Look, there's gonna be a blizzard, and this place's colder than an ice cube. I gotta get a fire going," Jonathan replied.

Maitland rocked to and fro on the cot, as if to private music. "Get out," he repeated, listlessly now.

Jonathan shrugged. Maitland could grumble all he wanted, but Jonathan didn't intend to leave until he had a fire started. Since there was no wood in the cabin, he'd have to seek it outside.

Outdoors, Jonathan quickly circled the shack. He'd seen firewood stacked against the foundations of other houses in the area, but he found none here.

Finally he spotted a couple of big branches not far from the house. He thought about chopping them up, but he didn't see an axe. He'd never used one anyway.

As he wrestled with the branches, Jonathan wondered what Barry would do in a spot like this. The answer came to him right away. Barry would go to town, get the sheriff, and say, "Drunk out there with no heat. Take care of it." Then Barry would tear out of this creepy town.

But that was Barry. Jonathan dragged two smaller branches into the house, breaking them with his hands.

"What's this?" Maitland asked.

"For the fire. You got a saw?"

"You're crazy," the man said.

Jonathan searched the cartons until he found one full of old, rusty tools. He grabbed a saw and attacked the branch.

Jonathan remembered that the last time he had used a saw, he'd been eight years old. Barry had tried to teach him about basic tools, but Jonathan had been so terrible at it that Barry teased him unmercifully.

Now, somehow, Jonathan managed to cut enough wood to make a fire. After bunching up some old newspapers in the fireplace, he piled the wood wigwam-style atop the papers. Then he threw a match in.

Instantly, the cabin filled with smoke. But then the fire caught and the smoke found the chimney. A fairly good fire was soon crackling. Its warmth spread like a smile around the room.

Jonathan was pleased with himself. It was the first time in his entire life he'd done the right thing in an emergency.

He turned to look at his father. Maitland was staring at the fire as if it were a ghost. Shadows from the flames struck his gaunt face and made him look even worse.

"So," Jonathan said briskly, "what do you do for food?"

Maitland sat up abruptly. "Who do you think you are? Get out of my place, do you hear me?"

"I just wanted to help."

The man stood, unsteadily. "Listen, you, go home. You got no business here. You got nothing to do with me. Go home."

Jonathan let anger cloak his hurt. Nothing he could do would reach this man! He slammed the door as he went outside.

By this time it was snowing hard, and the wind howled in his ears. He slogged through the wet, heavy snow to his VW.

As he started up the engine and began to back up, his tires slipped in the mud and snow. It was slick, but nothing the old bus couldn't handle.

Then, abruptly, Jonathan killed the engine. Gripping the wheel, he stared at the cabin. A minute later, with his sleeping bag in hand, he got out and returned to Maitland's shack.

When he stepped in the door, Maitland was still lying on his cot, staring at the ceiling. He turned as Jonathan came in.

"My VW is stuck," Jonathan lied. "Terrible storm out there." He went to the fire and fanned his hands over the warmth. His skin tingled happily.

"Why'd you ever have to come here in the first place?" the man groaned.

"To see you," Jonathan said. "I'll shovel the VW out tomorrow morning and be gone."

Maitland lay there silently. His chest rose and fell with his breathing, but that was the only sign of life. Though he was awake and glaring at the ceiling, he didn't say a thing.

Jonathan turned his own attention to the ceiling and noticed quite a few spider webs. He could imagine his mom's reaction to this place. She wouldn't want to spend five minutes here, especially with the spiders. Their home back in Heritage Hills looked great all the time. A magazine photographer could have stopped by anytime and just started snapping.

"Did you build this place?" Jonathan asked.

The man merely grunted. Jonathan didn't know if it was a yes or a no. Then Maitland reached under his cot for a brown bottle.

"You know, that stuff is bad for you, especially on an empty stomach," Jonathan commented. He looked at two cartons stacked atop each other near the icebox. He figured that's what passed for a cupboard around here. He rummaged through the cartons and found a few cans.

"Hey, why don't I heat up some of this? I'll bet you're hungry."

Maitland said nothing. Jonathan

figured that was the closest he was going to get to a yes. He began heating up a none-too-clean saucepan of pork and beans.

"You just move in and take charge, don't you?" Maitland grumbled.

"No. I've never done anything like this." Jonathan remembered another line from the counselor's evaluation. "A follower, not a leader. No real initiative."

Jonathan shrugged and looked at Maitland. He noticed how his father's dark eyebrows ran together, just like his did. Jonathan's half brother sometimes laughed and said, "You got eyebrows like a monkey!"

Just then, a mouse ran across the floor near Jonathan's sleeping bag. Jonathan's eyes followed it. He was fascinated. Imagine, a mouse lived in this cabin—maybe more than one.

Jonathan's mind went back to last summer when the Grants took a cabin at the lake. On the very first night, Mom saw a mouse.

"What a filthy place! There's a mouse

in here!" she cried in outrage.

"Well, they'll hear about this," Barry stormed.

"It's right there, right by my dressing table," Mom said, as if the mouse had ruined her living space.

They had gone directly to the manager of the place, got their money back, and hurried to a nice motel.

But here, in this place, a mouse seemed quite at home. This one cocked its head and seemed to exchange looks with Jonathan.

The smell of the bubbling pork and beans roused Jonathan. He found two bowls and brought one to Maitland. He didn't take it, so Jonathan set it on the floor beside him. Then Jonathan sat on the broken chair to eat.

He took a taste and said, "I've always liked pork and beans. We don't have it much at home. In fact, we rarely have simple stuff. Mom is a gourmet cook."

Maitland made no response. The pork and beans sat on the floor beside him, steaming.

"I, uh . . . don't like that fancy stuff Mom cooks." Jonathan thought it sounded weird, his own voice making all the noise. At last in irritation he asked, "Hey, what's it take to get a rise out of you?"

"Didn't ask you here. Didn't ask you for anything. You have to be stupid to stick around where you're not wanted."

"Yeah, well, my VW is stuck," Jonathan lied. "Believe you me, I'd go right now if I could. I mean, somebody'd have to be crazy to want to spend time with you."

"Well, maybe I'll just get a shovel and . . . " Maitland stumbled up, looked around, and found a shovel.

"You're in no shape to dig. Anyway, the storm's pretty bad."

"Don't tell me what kind of shape I'm in." Maitland turned an angry, flushed face to Jonathan, then rushed outside with the shovel.

Jonathan hurried after him. "Hey, knock it off, will you?" But Maitland continued to slash the snow around the VW's tires. Despite his frenzy, he was accomplishing nothing.

"Knock it off! You wanna get a heart attack or something?" Jonathan shouted.

"Leave me alone, will you?" Maitland was wheezing and coughing by now.

"You're just moving snow around, for Pete's sake!" Jonathan objected. He tried to grab the shovel, but Maitland gave him a push and Jonathan tumbled backwards into the snow. The fall didn't hurt, but for a minute he had the breath knocked out of him.

Maitland turned pale. "I didn't mean to . . . "

Jonathan scrambled up. "Yeah, sure. Hey, let's go inside huh? We're not gonna get this done tonight."

Maitland nodded dumbly. He started back to the cabin, using the shovel for support.

A funny new feeling came over Jonathan. He, Jonathan, was the adult here. Maitland was the child.

It was so different with Barry. When he wanted to help in the workshop, Barry would smile and say, "Hey, thanks a lot, Jon, but this work is pretty precise. I better handle it myself, okay?"

It was the same no matter what Jonathan tried to do. His parents only asked that he make them proud in school, but he couldn't even make the lousy football team. He had this funny, quirky personality, and he was clumsy. Jonathan just couldn't get over feeling stupid and useless all the time.

"All we want is for you to be a well-rounded, happy person. Nothing could make us prouder of you." That was the speech. Sometimes Mom gave it, sometimes Barry. Sometimes the words were changed, but never the meaning.

And lately those words were driving Jonathan crazy. They seemed to echo off the walls of his bedroom and follow him down the corridors. They seemed to mutter at him as he slept or when he drove. He couldn't shut them out anymore. Nor could he seem—as much as he tried—to make it come true.

"Do well in school," they asked.

"He's a bright guy, but he's just not motivated," the teachers said.

"Have fun in sports," they asked.

"Uncoordinated, no team spirit. Just doesn't seem to like sports," the coaches said.

"Be a well-rounded, happy person," they asked.

"Poorly adjusted, unsocial, a loner," said the counselor.

Fruit of a bad tree? Now inside the cabin, Jonathan turned and looked at Maitland. His father had grown quiet and almost appeared ashamed. Hunched over on his cot, he picked up the bowl of pork and beans and started eating. Finally, he looked at Jonathan and said, "I didn't mean to push you. God, you coulda fallen and hit your head!"

"I know you didn't mean to. Man, I roughhouse with my brother ten times harder than that. It's nothing."

Maitland at last looked—really looked—at Jonathan. "You know, you ain't got the ugly things about me. You only got what's not so bad. Like my eyes.

Always was my best feature. You got my eyes."

Jonathan smiled nervously, and settled uneasily on the broken chair. "I'm the only one in my family with blue eyes. I sorta feel like an outsider at times. I couldn't figure out why I had blue eyes and not even the grandparents did, or the cousins . . . "

Maitland licked his lips, seeming nervous, too. "Your mom writes regularly. That's good of her. She says you're doing okay. Says you're nothing like me. Always makes me glad to hear that." He gave a gravelly, bitter chuckle.

"I'm not sure who I'm like. Mom is really smart, you know. She can do the Sunday crossword easy. Sometimes even without a dictionary."

A glassy look came into Maitland's eyes. He seemed to be remembering moments from long ago. "When I knew your mom . . . why she was smart and all, but she was just a girl. So pretty, laughing . . . "

Jonathan leaned closer, feeling like a

little kid who is at last allowed to peek into a secret room he'd always wondered about. He wanted to hear every word. He longed to know how his parents met, what they'd thought and said, what they'd planned.

There must have been good things between them, if only for a little while. His mother acted as if every moment of it was awful. Still, Jonathan wanted to believe there was joy buried somewhere there.

"How'd you guys meet?" he gently asked.

Maitland shuddered and slumped on his cot. All the momentary liveliness was gone. His eyes turned dull again. "It's crazy to talk about it. You got your own family. Think about them."

"I came here because I want to know you. To talk to you. To understand, you know?"

"Nothin' to understand. I told you, I'm a bum."

"But before . . . "

"Who remembers before—or wants to?" Maitland stiffened and almost seemed angry again. "I'm surprised she let you come. She shouldn't have."

"I'm almost seventeen. I can visit my father if I want to," Jonathan said.

"I ain't your father. Grant is. What do you want to keep lying for?"

"You're my natural father. Don't you think I'm curious about that?"

Maitland stood up, quite steady on his feet. He was six feet tall, maybe a little more. "Curious? That what brought you? Well, all this little visit is gonna do is leave you with a sour memory.

"Me? I'm a liar and I drink too much. I live in this crummy shack, and I push a mop for what few dollars I need to live.

"I don't love nobody and nobody loves me. When little kids see this face of mine, sometimes they run and hide behind their mothers' skirts. I'm nothing to see and nothing to remember, boy. That's what curious got you."

Quietly Jonathan admitted, "It wasn't just curiosity. I came for another reason. I need somebody to help me."

The bloodshot eyes widened. "You

came to *me* for help?''

"It's no big trouble I'm in or anything. It's just that sometimes I'm scared to wake up in the morning . . . and scared of being an adult. Sometimes I'm just scared I'll never be good at anything."

Ed Maitland stood still for a moment. Then, suddenly, tears rushed down his face, catching in the crease of his scar.

4 THEY DIDN'T SAY much after that. Soon Maitland lay down on the cot, and Jonathan crawled into his sleeping bag on the floor. The only sound in the silent cabin was the crackling of the fire.

Before falling asleep, Jonathan took stock of the cabin again. He spotted cracks in the walls and places with knots the size of silver dollars.

The cabin sure needed a lot of work, Jonathan thought. Somebody should patch it and put up shelves to get those cartons off the floor.

Jonathan had often watched Barry build things. Now he thought, wouldn't it be something if he could fix this place up?

Jonathan planned to get up early in the morning. But when he awoke, bacon was already frying. "Smells good," he said as he rubbed the sleep out of his eyes.

Maitland had shaved and combed his hair. He looked almost respectable. "Thought I'd send you off with a good breakfast."

"Say, this place could use some repairs," Jonathan said, climbing out of his bag.

"It's just fine as it is."

"Cold seeps through those knots like flour through a sieve. I'd sure love to get some lumber and . . . "

"You a carpenter?" Maitland asked.

"Nah. But my stepdad does a lot of carpentry work. I'm always itching to help, but he never likes my work. Built a doghouse once, and he built a new one the next day. Put mine on the woodpile."

Maitland served the eggs and bacon, and Jonathan dug in.

"Hey, these just hit the spot." Jonathan paused for a moment, then returned to his earlier train of thought. "You know what? I'd like to try my hand at some carpentry around here. Just to see if I could do it."

Maitland blinked rapidly. "Thought you were going when you got the VW free."

"Yeah, but it'd be fun to hang around a few days. The family is going to Aspen.

They'd like me to go, but that bores me stiff.''

"Wouldn't fixing up this shack bore you, boy?"

"No." Jonathan began to grin. "I'd love to try this. Nobody would be hanging over my shoulder to say I wasn't doing it right."

"This place is all right the way it is," Maitland said. "Well, I gotta go to work."

Jonathan followed him out the door. The morning sky was bright blue, almost cloud-free. It was bitterly cold, and the snow looked icy and brittle. Icicles hung like inverted candles from the trees.

Jonathan pretended to shovel out the VW, then offered to drive Maitland into town. Maitland shrugged and took the offer.

It was awkward when Jonathan dropped him off in front of the small grocery store. Maitland thought this was goodbye, so he tried to be nice.

"Thanks for the ride, kid. Luck, huh?" Then he turned quickly and hurried into the building.

Jonathan was determined, however, that it wasn't going to be goodbye. He immediately sought out a phone and called home to say he'd be in Stony River for a few days.

"Are you getting along all right with Ed?" Jonathan's mother asked.

"Sure," Jonathan lied.

Running from the phone, he bumped into Liz Finch.

"Hey, Jonathan, you look like a cat with a saucer of cream," she said. "How come you're still in town?"

"I got together with my dad last night. I'm staying with him a couple of days. I'm gonna get some lumber and fix up the cabin."

"Honest? That's great."

"Yeah," Jonathan said.

"Well, I gotta go help my mom. I'll see you later."

"See you!" Jonathan called after her. She turned and waved.

His bitter feelings of yesterday gone, Jonathan realized he really liked Liz. He couldn't remember liking a girl at

Heritage Hills that much. Maybe it was just the mood he was in.

After a stop at the lumberyard, Jonathan returned to Maitland's cabin. Methodically, he began nailing up slats where the boards had separated from each other in the cabin. Barry called it weatherstripping.

When he finished his work, Jonathan stepped back and surveyed the little shack. It didn't look as great as if Barry had done it, but it looked okay. He put his hand on the wall and noted that he had stopped the icy wind from coming in.

Jonathan grinned and said to himself, "Looks okay, Jon." He laughed out loud. "Well, Barry, the old wood butcher didn't do half bad, huh?"

Next on his list were the shelves. He screwed the triangular brackets into the walls, then mounted the boards. One was a bit uneven. Yet they were sturdy, and Jonathan was able to put most of the cartons on them. Suddenly the miserable little shack started looking pretty good.

It was two in the afternoon before

Jonathan realized he was starving. He had worked through lunchtime. He jumped into his VW and drove to Finch's coffee shop for a sandwich.

"You been working hard?" Liz asked him.

"Yeah, and it's great. I guess I'm not as big an idiot as I thought."

Liz laughed her hearty laugh and Jonathan grinned. "You know, you're easier to talk to than any girl I know," he said. He blushed a little as he said it.

"Thanks."

Later, Jonathan asked Liz if she knew how his father got his scar.

"I think it was an accident in the Army. In Vietnam. You knew he served there?"

"No," Jonathan admitted.

"He doesn't talk about it, but I think it happened when he lost his foot."

"I didn't know about that either. He doesn't limp or anything."

"Yeah, I know. They fixed him up with something."

Jonathan wondered if his father was a

hero. Maybe he had even had a medal. Maybe his injury broke up his marriage. Maybe, maybe . . .

Jonathan finished his sandwich and went looking for his father. He found him mopping the bar floor.

For a moment Maitland just stared. Jonathan noticed his hands tighten on the mop handle. "You ain't gone yet?" he asked wearily.

"No. You finished work?"

"Yeah. So what?"

"So I thought maybe I could drive you home," Jonathan replied.

"I ain't done my drinking yet," Maitland replied.

"I sorta thought maybe this one time you could skip that," Jonathan hesitantly suggested.

Maitland sighed. Then with a mutter, he trudged out to the VW with Jonathan.

On the short drive to the cabin, Jonathan asked him, "What was it like in the Army?"

"That's ancient history."

"I was wondering how you got hurt,"

Jonathan said.

"A stinking, senseless accident. The truck turned over and spilled a bunch of us in a ravine. Me and another dogface got caught by the fire. He died and I got ugly."

"It must've been awful," Jonathan said quietly.

"I suppose you thought maybe I was some kind of hero, eh?"

"Maybe you were," Jonathan said. "Was Mom real upset about the injuries?"

"Your mother made the best of it. She makes the best of everything. You know that."

When they were near the cabin, Jonathan said, "You ever do any skilled work?"

"I'm one of those jack of all trades and master of none."

"Didn't you ever want to do anything special?"

"Look kid, what business is all this of yours?"

"You're my father. I'd just like to know

something about you."

"I keep telling you: Grant is your father."

Jonathan pulled up to the cabin door and killed the motor. "I don't know what I'll be. Maybe a carpenter. Jeff wants to be a doctor, and Gigi would like to be a lawyer. They never get scared like I do."

"Scared? Scared of what?" Maitland asked.

"Scared of not making it. I mean, Barry has so much. The big house, big car, vacations all over the world. He's thirty-nine years old and he's worth a small fortune. He did it all himself, too. How can I ever touch that kind of success?"

Maitland laughed a hollow laugh. "What do you expect from me? Permission to be a failure? Did you think I was the hero woodsman living in the wilderness, finding the true meaning of happiness? 'If a man does not keep pace with his companions, perhaps it is because he hears a different drummer.' Something like that?"

"That's Thoreau," Jonathan said.

"He's one of my favorite writers. Do you like Thoreau, too?"

Maitland seemed sorry he'd offered the quote. "I hate Thoreau. I think he was a fool. I think all writers are fools, idiots." His voice throbbed with anger.

Maitland went in the cabin a bit ahead of Jonathan. He stopped, thunderstruck. "Oh Lord." He stared at the weatherstripping and the shelves. "Did you do all this?"

"Yeah," Jonathan said. "I did it."

"You had no right," Maitland muttered.

"It's okay, isn't it? I mean, it's not a bad job?" Jonathan's heart pounded. His whole sense of worth hung on the man's words.

Maitland walked around the place. He shook his head. "Where'd you learn all this? I can't imagine a kid your age knowing how to do such stuff."

Jonathan felt warm, from the top of his head to the tips of his toes. For once in his life, he was proud of himself.

5 "I WAS THINKING," Jonathan said, "You could use a cupboard, too. I've never made a drawer, but I bet I could. I've got plenty of lumber left over."

He pulled a large-sized paperback book from his pocket. "I got this today at the lumberyard. The instructions are real easy. The drawers have to have glides, you know?"

Maitland put his face in his hands. He sat like that for several seconds. Then he accidentally kicked over one of the bottles he kept under his cot. "See what you made me do?" he angrily demanded of Jonathan.

"Sorry."

"I want you to go, boy. *Now.*"

"Couldn't I just finish the cupboard?"

Maitland looked at the tall, big-shouldered boy. His hair was dark and thick, like Maitland's at that age. He had innocent blue eyes and a gentle smile.

"Look, boy," Maitland said with a new softness in his voice, "you go home. It's a wonderful place for you, that Heritage Hills.

"Believe me, good things happen to people who live in places like that. They go to college. They get good jobs, and their dreams come true. Success begets success.

"Failure is like that, too. It's contagious. I got it, boy. Don't you catch it, too, you hear?"

Jonathan deliberately ignored the warning. He came closer and said, "That word—'beget.' It's from the Bible, right? Bet you've read that and plenty of other books, too."

He paused and then awkwardly blurted out, "I like books. I hate school, but I love books. I like to go somewhere quiet with a book and read for hours. I bet you do, too."

Maitland protested. "You're crazy boy. I'm not an educated man. I'm ignorant."

"Maybe you aren't educated, but an ignorant man couldn't quote Thoreau like you did." Jonathan smiled and said, "I think I'll go out and chop some firewood for us. Gonna be a cold night."

Jonathan took the axe he bought at the

lumberyard and went outside. He gathered some wood and was just about to begin chopping when he heard Maitland cry, "Look out!" Jonathan lowered the axe and turned.

"Ain't you ever used an axe before?" Maitland asked.

"Nope."

"Well, let me show you how before you lose a leg!"

Maitland demonstrated how Jonathan should hold the tool and swing safely. "Use an axe like it's an extension of your own arm. The strokes should be smooth and easy," he explained.

Fairly quickly Jonathan was chopping wood with reasonable skill. The two of them worked until they made quite a pile.

Jonathan didn't pause as he chopped away, but once or twice he stole a look at the man beside him. How effortlessly Maitland worked, as if he did this everyday.

To Jonathan there was a special music in their working side by side. If a stranger had passed by, he'd think here was a real father and son who enjoyed doing chores together.

As they carried the wood inside, Jonathan noticed a little slip of paper lying on the floor. It had spilled from one of the cartons. As he stooped and picked it up, he innocently asked, "What's this?"

Maitland recognized the paper right away. With ferocious speed, he ripped it out of Jonathan's hands and pitched it into the fire. It was as though Jonathan had found something dirty and shameful.

For a second the man was quiet. Then he said, "Nothing. Just one of those slips the magazines send you when you mail them a piece they don't want."

Jonathan stared at him, wide-eyed. "You mean you're a *writer*?"

"I mean I'm a fool."

"I think it's great to write something and try to get it published."

"It don't mean a thing if they don't publish it."

"Could I see some of your stuff?"

"No," the man snapped.

Jonathan let the subject drop while he

helped fix the meal. But when they sat down to their hamburgers and coffee, he volunteered, "Sometimes I think I'd like to be a writer. I'd sure like to read some of your stuff."

"No," Maitland said again. He drank his coffee so fast that some spilled on his chin.

"What kind of things do you write?"

"Garbage," Maitland retorted.

"I mean, fiction or articles and like that?"

Maitland frowned. "Just plain garbage. The ramblings of a lunatic. 'Full of sound and fury signifying nothing.' "

"*Macbeth*!" Jonathan exclaimed.

"Lord have mercy on this poor fool," Maitland groaned.

"Do you write plays?"

"No. This is what I write." Maitland got up, walked to the bookshelves, and yanked a carton down. It was packed full of yellow envelopes.

With an angry jerk, Maitland turned the box upside down, spilling the contents onto the floor. Dozens of envelopes spilled at Jonathan's feet. "Here they are, the whole miserable lot of them. Only thing they're good for now is kindling."

Eagerly, Jonathan sat down on the floor and, opening the first envelope he picked up, began to read the article inside. That one finished, he chased through the next, and the next . . .

They were short articles, all about nature. Like seeing a nighthawk at dawn, or hearing the booming sound a bird makes when it dives. Others described the browsing deer or how to test the hardness of ice on a winter pond. All of them throbbed with the sights, sounds, and smells of nature at Stony River.

As Jonathan read, he got a lump in his throat. He was deeply impressed, but he had enough sense not to tell that to the angry man now lying on his cot.

"It's good stuff," he simply commented when he had finished.

"Shows what you know," the man growled.

The reason for Maitland's bitterness was all too apparent. The envelopes were full of rejection slips from the best magazines in the country. Jonathan shook his head sadly.

* * *

In the morning, Jonathan drove Maitland into town again.

"You'll be going home this afternoon, right?" Maitland asked him.

"Looks like," Jonathan said. But he had no such intention.

He was whistling as he went into the lumberyard and ran into one of the first men he had seen in Stony River—the railroad cap. "So you're really Maitland's kid, eh?" the old man said with a chuckle.

"Yep."

"I'll be darned. I thought you were a city punk come to raise some Cain."

The old man helped Jonathan pick out the lumber he needed for the cupboard. Then he threw in the hardware at cost. "Glad you're doing something nice for Ed," he said. "Lots of us tried, but he's so proud."

"Yeah," Jonathan said. "He really doesn't want my help either."

"Well, you got plenty of sand, young fella. Standing up to Ed. He's always helping out—like when we had the forest fire. He worked without sleep for a week to save other folks' houses. Always wanted to repay him, but he wouldn't take nothing."

As he paid for his purchases, Jonathan noticed a painting on the wall. It was of a circling hawk. It reminded him of his father's pieces.

On his way out, Jonathan picked up a copy of the local paper, the *Southwest Courier*.

Back at the cabin, he finished half of the cupboard, then stopped to read the paper. After browsing through the reports and articles, he decided that the *Courier* just might be the kind of paper that would print good stories by a local author.

By early that afternoon, Jonathan had finished sanding the cupboard. Hungry and satisfied with his job, he headed for Finch's cafe.

At the coffee shop, he called the editor

of the paper. "Look, would you like to see a couple of articles about local birds and nature . . . that kind of thing?"

"We don't use that type of article," the man replied gruffly.

"But these stories are just like Thoreau's."

There was a pause. "Yeah? Who says?"

"They're the work of a local, uh, a sort of local philosopher."

"Well, tell your philosopher to send some samples to me. I doubt if I can use 'em, but I'll take a look. And tell him to send a self-addressed stamped envelope so I can send it all back."

"Thanks," Jonathan said.

Jonathan picked out his three favorite articles and sent them in, using Liz Finch's address. He knew better than to clear it with Maitland. His father would undoubtedly accuse Jonathan of butting in again.

"You staying in town a little longer?" Liz asked Jonathan when he returned to the table.

"A few days maybe."

"Can you come to our Christmas party Friday night?"

Jonathan looked hard at the girl. She was smiling as if she liked Jonathan. The girls at Heritage High didn't smile at him like this. "If I'm here, I'll come, Liz."

"Great," she said.

When Maitland came up to Jonathan's VW after work, he had a package. It was nicely wrapped, and he thrust it at Jonathan. "It's sort of a goodbye present, boy."

Jonathan remembered that today was the day he was supposed to go. He unwrapped the gift and then stared. He couldn't believe his eyes. It was a leather-bound copy of *Life in the Woods* by Thoreau.

6 "THIS IS WONDERFUL," Jonathan said softly. "Thanks, Dad. Thanks a lot."

"It's not much. I doesn't begin to pay you for the work you've done."

Jonathan could hardly wait for the look on Maitland's face when he saw the cupboard. He hadn't felt like this since he was a little kid bringing back that leather belt he'd made for Barry at summer camp. He'd even carved a big BG on it. Barry had said it was wonderful, but he never wore it.

That had hurt Jonathan. Barry thought the belt was rotten, like everything else Jonathan made or did.

"Man alive!" Maitland gasped when he entered the cabin. He pulled open a cupboard drawer. "Smooth as silk! You're incredible."

"I was glad to do it. It was fun. It really was."

"Well . . . now you're going, eh?"

"I thought I'd wait till after supper. I got a pizza for us. It needs to be warmed in the oven."

Maitland looked out the window. "Storm clouds building. Might be best if you started now."

"Oh, there's plenty of time," Jonathan reassured him.

While they were eating the pizza, Jonathan said, "Liz Finch asked me to the Christmas party Friday."

"Bet you go to plenty of parties back home. Your mom said you were pretty popular."

"I'm not. In fact, it's real hard for me to make friends."

"You're a good-looking kid," Maitland argued.

"I'm just average. I'm nothing special back home. At Heritage Hills High, all the kids are good-looking. Plus they're good in sports and have got great personalities.

"You know," Jonathan continued, "I think the parents must hide their dumb-looking, stupid kids in attics or something. I never see any of them at school. I seem to be the only jerk there."

"That's nonsense!" Maitland was

almost yelling. "It's all in your head. You're as good as any of them. Better!"

The words meant more to Jonathan because it suddenly struck him that his father was stone-cold sober. It was the first time Jonathan had seen him like that.

A sprinkling of snow began to dust the window. "Hey, looks like you were right," Jonathan declared. "It's snowing already. Maybe I ought to wait till morning to go."

Maitland laughed. It was the first time Jonathan had heard a warm, genuine laugh from him. Maitland had begun to see just what Jonathan was up to, and it amused him.

The next morning, after dropping his father off, Jonathan went to Finch's cafe. As he ate breakfast, Mr. Finch approached him and sat down.

"Jonathan," he began, "I thought you'd like to know what I heard yesterday. Alf Sanders—he runs the bar—said he hasn't seen Maitland sober in eight years. But he was sober yesterday."

Jonathan smiled.

Mr. Finch went on. "I wanted to tell you something about your dad, Jonathan. See, a few years back, I had a run of bad luck. The wife was sick, then I busted my leg.

"Well, Ed knew I was in trouble, so he came in every morning and ran the gas pumps. He even did some mechanical work.

"He's no great shakes at it, but he did all right. I couldn't have made it without him."

"Thanks for telling me," Jonathan said. Mr. Finch nodded and walked off.

After finishing his meal, Jonathan called home.

"I don't know when I'll be getting back, Mom."

"Jon, I don't understand. We're leaving for Aspen on Sunday."

"I've just got some things to do."

"Are you in trouble or what?"

"No, Mom."

"You're probably just making a nuisance of yourself. You have a way of doing that sometimes, honey."

"Yeah, Mom. Look, I'll try to make it back on Saturday."

"All right," she said. "Jeff will pack your things for Aspen." She sighed then and asked, "How is Ed?"

"He's okay, Mom."

"Are you staying with him?"

"Yeah."

"You mean he's *letting* you stay with him?"

"Sort of," Jonathan said.

"Is he drunk a lot? You know, honey, it worries me that you're staying with a man who drinks too much. I never told you what a drinker he was because I didn't want to burden you with a lot of rubbish, but . . ."

"He stopped drinking, Mom," Jonathan said.

"Really?" His mother was silent for a moment. Then she added, "Well, that's a surprise."

"Yeah."

"What does he do for a living, Jon?"

Jonathan swallowed. "Oh, this and

that. He's a pretty fair mechanic."

"I remember when he couldn't even change the oil on our car properly."

"I guess he's changed."

"It sounds like it. Well, do try to hurry home, will you? After all, you're probably just in the way up there. Remember when you stayed with Uncle Clyde last summer, and he said he couldn't get a thing done? You were always underfoot, but he was too polite to ask you to go home."

"Yeah, I remember, Mom."

"And then you hung around that cabinetmaker's shop, and he had to call us . . . "

"Yeah, I remember, Mom. For Pete's sake, that was five years ago!" Jonathan felt his hands balling into fists.

"Well, just don't make a pest of yourself. We could use you here to help pack for Aspen."

"I don't pack so good either, Mom," Jonathan said, his voice trembling a little. "You remember Barry always has to repack my bags for me?"

Jonathan's mother laughed, but

Jonathan didn't. He just said goodbye
and hung up.

When he returned to his table, he found
Liz refilling the salt and pepper shakers.
"You look peeved," she remarked.

"Yeah. Mom thinks I'm four years old,
still too dumb to put my coat on right."

Liz laughed, which brought a lovely
pink flush to her face. Jonathan just
stared. He loved watching her quick smile
and dancing eyebrows.

"You can make our party, huh,
Jonathan?" she asked.

"Yeah."

"It's not really a big deal. We sing
Christmas carols, eat fruitcake, and drink
cider. Then we draw tiny gifts from a
barrel."

"Tell me what kind of gift to bring."

"Oh, just some little thing. Everybody
just makes a gift and drops it in the barrel. Then we reach in and take something.
You can buy anything, a tree ornament
or something."

"Sounds   like   fun.   Uh . . . is
there . . . like dancing?"

Liz grinned. "I can't dance. Isn't that terrible?"

"You can't? Me neither," Jonathan admitted.

"Then I guess we'll just eat fruitcake and talk, huh?" Liz said.

"Yeah." Jonathan smiled.

Jonathan went to his father's last stop, the bar, to pick him up. At first he didn't find him there. But then he heard rowdy laughter from the back room and went to explore. He found Maitland there drinking with Henry Stohlman, the man who'd spat tobacco juice that first day.

Maitland turned when he saw Jonathan. "I'll see you out at the cabin, boy."

"Oh, I figured I'd give you a ride."

"We got some serious drinking to do," Maitland said. "It's Henry's birthday."

Jonathan was disappointed to see that Maitland was already a little drunk. He'd figured maybe his father had turned a corner. And he was proud that maybe he'd played a part in that. "But, uh, it might snow," Jonathan argued.

"Git," Maitland said simply.

"Yeah, you ain't dry behind the ears yet," the old man snapped.

Jonathan glared at the tobacco chewer. Henry Stohlman saw the hatred in the boy's eyes. He spat a stream of tobacco juice right at Jonathan's shoes. It was a direct hit. He roared with laughter. He was preparing to spit again when Jonathan whirled on his heels and left.

"Dirty old coot," Jonathan said to the bartender as he walked past.

The bartender darkened. "You got no respect for your elders, boy?"

"Respect for Henry Stohlman, that old fool?"

"Henry's a good man. When this town hit hard times, he loaned a lot of people the money to feed their families."

"He's in there getting my father drunk!"

"Nobody gets your father drunk. Ed drinks when he wants to. He's his own man."

Jonathan strode outside, remembering what he'd told his mother about Maitland not drinking anymore. What a laugh! He should have said Maitland was the same old drunk he'd always been.

Jonathan kicked the VW into motion and drove out to the cabin. It was clear, but bitterly cold. If Maitland stumbled and fell into a snowbank, he could freeze to death.

Jonathan stood at the window and looked up at the stars. He kept telling himself that Maitland was nothing to him. What was a biological father if you never saw him? What did it matter if he fell into the snow and died?

It surely wouldn't be Jonathan's fault. He'd come here and tried to make it better for the guy.

And how did Maitland show his appreciation? He sat around drinking with Henry Stohlman, that's what, instead of spending time with the son he'd neglected for sixteen years.

Jonathan stuck his hands in his pockets and stared at the fire. His eyes roamed the cabin, finally settling on his copy of *Life in the Woods.*

Big deal, Jonathan thought. Some father. He gives me a lousy book and figures we're even.

Jonathan snatched up the book, fully intending to pitch it into the fire. But as he did so, it fell open in his hands. He saw there for the first time what the man had scrawled on the inside cover.

To Jonathan: Believe it or not, I always cared.

Ed Maitland.

He'd written that when he thought Jonathan was leaving. It would probably embarrass him now. Still, there it was.

Jonathan tucked the book into his sleeping bag and got ready to go look for his father. But the moment he opened the door, Maitland came through it.

"Where you going, boy?" he asked.

"I was going to look for you."

"Well, nobody—especially no kid— needs to look for Ed Maitland." He came swaggering in.

Jonathan took a good look at his father

as he passed into the cabin. He recognized that Maitland was handsome—even with the scar—in a rough, wild kind of way. Jonathan could imagine his mother going temporarily crazy over him.

Of course, it didn't work. It was probably doomed to fail from the start. Yet Jonathan could see how his mother had come to like Ed Maitland. Jonathan liked him, too.

7

ON FRIDAY MORNING, Jonathan said, "Why don't you come to the Christmas party with me tonight?"

Maitland, busy scrambling the eggs, laughed. "Not a chance."

"How come? Don't you get lonely sometimes and want to be with people?"

"Nope."

"What kinda family did you grow up in?"

"Boy, ain't we full of questions this morning!" He filled Jonathan's plate with fluffy scrambled eggs.

"Well, your parents were my grandparents, so I'm curious."

Maitland sat down with his own plate. "You got grandparents on your mother's side. How many grandparents you need, boy? Anyway, they're dead. I didn't even know them."

"You were an orphan?" Jonathan asked.

"Orphan? That's a word I never applied to myself."

"But when did your parents die?"

Maitland put down his fork. "Know what, boy? You're bound to be a big success in life. You know why? You're persistent. You get your mind set on something and you don't quit.

"Okay, okay, about my parents. They were both dead by the time I was thirteen. I had a decent foster home till I was seventeen. Then the Army adopted me."

Maitland scowled, "Now don't go whining about my bad breaks or, so help me, I'll fling you right into Stony River."

Jonathan laughed. "I still wish you'd come with me tonight. I bet you'd enjoy it."

"You want me trapped in some ladderback chair, balancing a dish of fancy little cookies and ice cream? Watching some fool playing Santa Claus? And the likes of Mrs. Finch telling me I don't look so good? Why, the kind of friends I value, they're right here in the woods."

"You got friends in the woods?"

"Sure." Maitland gathered up the empty breakfast dishes, then pulled his coat off a hook on the wall. "Come on. I'll show you."

Jonathan trailed him outside. A bright sun shone, and the air was warmer than yesterday. They crunched across the snow until a flurry of sound near the edge of the still, half-frozen lake made Jonathan turn.

"Mallards," Maitland said. "Handsome birds. And they got big appetites, so they keep the mosquitoes down real nice.

"Some people complain 'cause they squawk and holler louder than most anything. But none of those mallards ever found fault with me. Friends of mine, they are. Don't mind if I'm shaved or not."

They kept on walking. Jonathan spotted a strange bird with a long bill and a reddish head. It looked like a duck with a woodpecker's head.

"Don't see too many of them. That's a female there; redhead. Everybody calls them fish ducks. Not all that common in the winter time, so I count myself lucky to see one. It's special. That's a merganser."

A metallic chip-chip-chip sound came from the branches of a tree and Maitland looked up. "There. My yellow-rumped warbler. You'll catch him hanging upside down sometimes. Winter doesn't bother this bird."

"Doesn't look like a yellow rump to me," Jonathan said.

"He's wearing his winter clothes, boy. By summer he's yellow as egg yolk, and he sings a song sweeter than any you'll hear. Goes like this: chee-chee-chee-ah-wee."

"How about the squirrels," Jonathan asked. "I haven't seen any of them."

"You think a squirrel is fool enough to mess with winter? Different with the birds. They got good insulation.

"But the squirrel—no sir. He's down in his burrow. Walk lightly now, boy, 'cause we're probably stomping on his ceiling. Your squirrel is fat and sleek and fast asleep."

Something white flashed across the snow.

"Hare. Got his white coat for winter.

He's got snowshoes, too. Does all right,"
Maitland commented. "If you'd not been
here, he might've stopped for a chat. I got
a good passing relationship with a hare
or two. Real nice fellas."

Jonathan smiled. "Yeah, but people
need people."

"Nah. Get close to people, why, they
try to change you. Or else they get mad
at you 'cause you won't change. Now, I
never tried to get a merganser to change
his feathers, and no bird ever tried to re-
arrange me either."

* * *

Jonathan went to the Christmas party
at seven. It was held in the biggest room
in town, the lumber barn. Everything was
moved to the side. Scattered throughout
the room stood live Christmas trees in
pots, trimmed with gingerbread men and
popcorn strings.

Liz introduced Jonathan to a lot of people. But he felt ill at ease, just as he
always did when he met new faces.

He was glad to finally settle in a cozy
corner with Liz. The last girl he'd been

out with was Carla Lohman back home.
The only reason she had agreed to date
him was to make her boyfriend jealous.

"You, uh, got a boyfriend, Liz?"
Jonathan asked.

"No. I like the guy who's in our school
play, but just as a friend."

"Back home, kids sorta, you know,
start going steady in junior high already.
It makes you feel weird if you don't,"
Jonathan confessed.

Jonathan and Liz finished their fruitcake and went outside into the crisp, cool
night. The moon was a pale pearl-gray,
except for patches of dark spots.

Liz took up the thread of conversation.
"Around here, we don't pair off so early."

Jonathan grimaced. "Good old
Heritage Hills High. Even at a dance,
people think you're dumb if you hang
around. You're supposed to go off, the
two of you. If you don't, then the other
kids think you're an idiot or something."

Liz shrugged. "I'd hate to have to do
things a certain way just to satisfy
everybody else."

"Well, that's how it is in Heritage Hills. You gotta do certain things at a certain time or they make fun of you. If you're not doing real great with girls, they'll call you names."

Jonathan looked down at the slushy snow and mumbled, half hoping Liz wouldn't hear him. "I'm not . . . you know, real popular with girls. They . . . uh . . . think I'm stupid or something, I don't know."

Liz was looking right at him. "Maybe *they're* stupid."

Jonathan felt his skin turn red and warm. But her smile made him feel better. It was funny. He had known Liz for just a few days, but talking to her was nicer than talking to anybody he'd ever known.

"Liz, I . . . uh, I wish you were in Heritage Hills."

"I don't think I'd like it," Liz said. "But I like you."

"You do? Really? I mean . . . "

Liz laughed her big, throaty laugh. "Really."

Jonathan stared up at the moon. His brother was two years younger, but Jeff had twice his poise. He could go on a date and seem like a college guy. Jonathan always felt like a fool.

"Jonathan," Liz said.

He turned. "Yeah?"

She held a small bit of mistletoe over her head. "Look. It's mistletoe."

Jonathan stared at her. How beautiful she was! How he longed to kiss her. She wanted it, too, or she wouldn't be holding the mistletoe. But he couldn't make himself reach out for her.

Then Liz moved the mistletoe towards Jonathan. "Oh-oh," she whispered. "It's over your head now." Liz put her arms around his neck, brought his face to hers, and kissed him.

As she gently broke off the kiss, Jonathan felt a big smile break over his face.

"You're beautiful," he mumbled.

"Thanks."

"You're the most beautiful girl I've ever seen."

"Wow."

"You're so much prettier than those little snobs at Heritage High. You really put them in the shade, Liz," Jonathan declared warmly.

"It's the apples," Liz assured.

"What?"

"The apples. It makes our cheeks nice. All the girls in Stony River have apple cheeks. Very attractive."

For a moment Jonathan stared at her. Then they both laughed. They stumbled against each other, laughing until tears streamed down their faces.

Jonathan hated for that evening to end. And it wasn't just parting from Liz. Jonathan dreaded the next day. He had promised his mother he'd head back, but he couldn't. He couldn't bear the thought of another holiday at Aspen.

Last Christmas was a nightmare. There had been six families from Heritage Hills, all with kids about Jonathan's age, all gliding down the hills like Olympians.

Jonathan couldn't, for the life of him, learn to ski. The rest of them laughed every time he took a spill. Barry took Jonathan aside for a serious father-son talk.

"Look, Jon, don't let them stick you with this klutz label. Go out there and show them you can ski with the best of them. Go on. You can do it," he'd said.

So Jonathan ended up taking ski lessons from a guy named Huldreich, a big blond who claimed to be from Switzerland. Huldreich could get little kids looking good on the slopes in no time.

But no matter how hard he tried, Jonathan ended up with his feet in the air every time. After awhile, Huldreich began to mutter in foreign words that sounded like Swiss curses.

And now they wanted him to return to Aspen with the same people. He'd probably even get roped into another set of lessons from poor Huldreich!

As he said good night to Liz and drove to the cabin, it started to storm. But it was rain that fell, not snow. By the time Jonathan reached Maitland's cabin, the drops had turned into a steady downpour.

"Bad time for rain," Maitland said.

"How come?" Jonathan asked.

"It can flood. When the winter turns warm on you and a bunch of storms come through, the rivers overflow in the low lying places. It can be bad news."

"What do you do about it?" Jonathan wondered.

"If it looks bad, sandbag. Houses are built all along the Stony River, and they're all in danger. Happened before, maybe ten years ago. Sandbags were all that saved a couple of dozen homes. The Cornings, the Andersons, the Finches—them and more."

Jonathan's mind fixed on just one of those names. The Finches. Liz. He didn't sleep much that night.

By morning, the downpour had grown worse, with lightning bolts piercing a black sky.

"You picked a smart time to be getting out of here," Maitland said. "Best you get going right away."

Jonathan stared at his father. He

couldn't leave now—now of all times.
Trouble was coming, and he should be
here to help out.

Suddenly Jonathan realized how much
he cared about Stony River.

8 "I'D THINK EVERY guy on the sandbag line would count," Jonathan said, watching Maitland gather shovels.

"You ever do such a thing before?"

"No, but I could learn if you showed me."

"Jonathan," he said. It was the first time he'd ever used his son's name. "Your mother is going to wonder about you. She'll worry. Maybe you'd better go."

"I want to help here. I want to fill sandbags. I want to do this more than I've ever wanted to do anything."

The man shrugged and let Jonathan help him load the gear into the back of the VW. After parking at the hardware store, Jonathan dashed to the coffee shop to make a quick phone call to his mother.

"It's started to rain heavy, Mom. The roads are slick. I think I'd better stay over." He'd decided not to mention the flood and the sandbags.

"Jon, we're leaving for Aspen tomorrow."

"I'll head home when you guys get

back. Don't worry about me, I'll be all right. And you'll get along fine without me. We'll have our family Christmas when I get back. Okay?"

"Oh, honey, I don't know!"

"It'll be okay, Mom," Jonathan hastily reassured her. After promising five times to take care of himself, she reluctantly gave in.

Jonathan joined Maitland, helping load empty grain sacks into his VW. He was surprised to see other people—strangers to him—throwing sacks in, too. Occasionally they'd all pause and look at the threatening sky. Then, they'd work a little faster.

The Finches—the whole family—were already at Stony River filling sandbags when Jonathan and his father arrived. Though Liz was muddy and wet, she greeted Jonathan with a warm smile. That smile was worth more than any words of gratitude.

Maitland showed Jonathan the best way to shovel sand into the sacks. Then he taught him how to hoist the bags from person to person, sending the sacks to places where they'd do the most good.

As he labored away, Jonathan rarely paused to catch his breath. He was surprised by his own strength. He'd been so terrible at sports that he'd believed the coach's frustrated gripe, "You're a weakling, Grant!" Now he was keeping pace with grown men on the sandbag line.

From his vantage point on the riverbank, Jonathan had a clear view of the houses they were trying to save. Though most of them were well kept, none reflected much wealth. In fact, most garages in Heritage Hills were fancier! And yet the little houses seemed precious in a way the houses in Heritage Hills could never be.

Liz saw Jonathan's glance and explained. "We built those houses. Or at least, our fathers and grandfathers did. Mom and I helped build our porch two summers ago. I'd sure hate to see it go."

They broke for hot coffee and rolls. Jonathan and Liz sat together on a log, ignoring the rain which plastered the hair to their heads.

"We'll save the houses," Jonathan said, shocked at his confidence. He usually wasn't much for confidence, especially in himself.

"Yeah," Liz agreed. "I think we will at that."

Jonathan was amazed at how pretty she looked, even with her rain-soaked hair and muddy face. Jonathan tried to picture mud on Gigi's face. Then he tried to imagine mud on the faces of the girls at Heritage High who always looked perfect and smelled so nice. He couldn't.

Jonathan finished his roll and gulped his coffee. He didn't smell so good. None of the men did. None of the women did, either. But it didn't matter anymore.

"It's amazing how everybody turned out to help," Jonathan said. "Do you have a siren to call them or what?"

"When it rains like this, everyone just automatically comes to the houses in danger."

"Even if their own houses are on high ground?"

"Sure," Liz said. "Your father's house is on high ground and he's here. So are you."

She smiled and added, "Oh, we're not saints, Jonathan, don't get me wrong. We fight and holler same as other people. But when there's trouble, most of us are willing to help."

They went back to work, filling sandbags the whole day. By dusk, they'd done all they could.

"They say God helps those who help themselves," Liz said. "Well, we've done all we can. I guess the rest is up to Him."

"It's gonna be fine," Jonathan said, giving Liz's shoulders a little squeeze.

She grinned at him as she wiped the mud off her nose. "Are you always such a together guy, Jonathan?"

"No. Only in floods."

Not until he was back at Maitland's cabin that night did Jonathan realize how blistered his hands were.

"Look at you. The palms of your hands look like raw hamburger," Maitland said.

"I didn't feel it happening."

"Sit down here," Maitland ordered. He filled a basin with hot, soapy water and then scrubbed out the grimy wounds. Finally, he applied salve and bandages. Jonathan was surprised at his gentleness.

"Think we stopped the river from taking the houses?" Jonathan asked, listening to the roar of thunder.

"We tried. But that ain't always enough. Sandbags don't always work, and dreams don't always fly."

Maitland went to his cot. Before he lay down, he took a drink from his bottle. It was just one drink, though.

Jonathan crawled into his sleeping bag and tried to ignore the rain pounding on the roof.

Sometime during the night, it got cold. Bitterly cold. He woke up to a terrible gust of wind. Opening his eyes, he saw Maitland standing in the doorway, staring outside.

"It's freezing!" Jonathan groaned.

"It's snowing, boy. Ain't it beautiful?"

Jonathan got out of his bag and pulled a coat on. Then he joined his father at the door.

"Hey, look at it," Jonathan spoke in quiet wonder.

"Means that old river's stopped cold. Our sandbags made her pause. Now the snow'll hold her fast.

"Know what that means, boy? Means we saved all those houses, you and me and the rest. The river would've taken 'em down last night and left all those folks homeless. We did it, boy!"

He grinned and gave Jonathan a shove. "Get dressed. I want to build a snowman."

"At this hour?"

"You poor fool, it's almost dawn!"

Jonathan got dressed. By the time they got outside, there was a pink glow on the new snow.

Maitland dug in immediately by madly pushing a small snowball up a hill. Jonathan pushed another. Soon they had both the body and head formed.

As a finishing touch, Maitland set a tattered hat atop the head and wrapped a moth-eaten scarf around the neck.

Jonathan made the face from cinders.

"He looks like me," Maitland chuckled.

Laughing in return, Jonathan threw a snowball at the snowman. He missed the snowman, but hit Maitland right on target. Maitland returned the favor.

After they'd had enough, they went inside and cooked steaming oatmeal for breakfast.

"Did you ever make a snowman with Barry Grant, Jonathan?" Maitland asked.

"Sure."

"Good; that's good. I never met him, but I think he must be a decent man from what your mother says."

"Yeah, he is."

"Did he teach you how to ride a two-wheeler?"

"Yeah," Jonathan said. "Come to think of it, it's the only thing he ever taught me that I could do right."

Maitland grinned. He looked boyish when he grinned. "Suppose he taught you how to play baseball?"

"He tried, but I was the worst Little

Leaguer on the team. I almost drove the coach crazy."

"Did he razz you for that? Barry Grant, I mean?"

"No. He just looked sad. That's all he ever did. Just looked sad . . . and disappointed. I don't think razzing would've hurt as much."

Jonathan finished breakfast and glanced at the ragged old calendar on the wall. "Well, Thursday is Christmas. What do you do for Christmas?"

Maitland sneered. "I get drunk. And if I'm lucky, I sleep right through Christmas and never know it."

Jonathan shook his head. "My family makes a big deal out of Christmas. Barry puts up decorations before Thanksgiving. When I left last week, the tree was up with all the gifts underneath. It's one of those plastic trees so it never dies. Course it never lived either.

"And we've already had about ten Christmas parties. That's why it's not so bad missing Christmas with them. It seems like it's been Christmas for weeks!"

"Well, I never put up a tree," Maitland said.

"Didn't you ever want to?"

He shook his head. "What for? Say, I hope I'm not disappointing you. You probably thought I'd hike out into the woods and find us a sturdy little pine. Drag it in here and maybe fetch out some homemade ornaments."

"No, I didn't think that. But it doesn't seem right not to celebrate Christmas at all."

"Why should somebody pretend they're happy just because it's Christmas? That's just bunk." Maitland seemed angry. "If you're miserable for eleven months, why make believe you're happy at the end of December?"

Jonathan grimaced. "Why do you have to be so miserable all the time?"

"Well, maybe I ain't. Then again, maybe I am."

Maitland paused and then grumbled, "You got more talk in you than a wind-up toy. If you want a big Christmas, then head on home. You still got time. So go on, git."

Jonathan couldn't help but smile. His father seemed mad that Jonathan would go home and leave him alone on Christmas. He'd never admit to that, but there it was.

"I can't leave," Jonathan said. "What if it got warm again and the rain came? You might need me to help fill more sandbags."

Maitland shook his head. "You're one strange boy. I can't make head nor tail of you."

Jonathan laughed. "I can't either."

9 FOR A FEW days, the people of Stony River left the sandbags in place, just in case. But it turned out there was no need to worry. On Sunday afternoon, as Jonathan strolled with Liz along the riverbanks, everything seemed calm.

"Look, this is where it wanted to come surging over," Liz pointed out. "It would've taken the sheds and the barn and that porch for sure."

"I'm glad we stopped it," Jonathan said.

Liz nodded. Then, struck by a sudden thought, she turned to him. "Hey, Jon, it's Sunday and you didn't go home."

"Yeah. To tell you the truth, Liz, I hate to leave here. I mean, for the first time in my life, I don't feel like a jerk. I feel like . . . well, I'm useful or something.

"Last year, Jeff and I had this big fight. He ended it by hollering, 'Who needs you?' And I thought, yeah, he's right. Nobody needs me."

"Oh, Jon," Liz protested. "I'm sure your parents and your family need you and love you."

"I know they love me. And I love them. I'd do anything in the world for them. The trouble is . . . I can't *please* them. Pleasing them is like getting to the top of a steep glass mountain. All my life I've been climbing and slipping, climbing and slipping . . . "

Mrs. Finch looked out the door and shouted, "Jonathan, there's a phone call for you."

When Jonathan got inside, Mrs. Finch said, "It's an editor from the newspaper. Did you give our phone number to someone down at the *Courier*?"

"Oh yeah. I gave him this address and phone number." Jonathan picked up the phone.

"Is this Ed Maitland?" a man asked.

"No, I'm his kid. I sent the articles in for him. Is that what you're calling about?"

"Yeah. Say, I think we can use all three of those pieces you sent in. Would fifty bucks apiece be okay? I'd like to run the one on the antelope for this week's

Christmas issue."

Jonathan felt dizzy. This man was acting so matter-of-fact, as though this happened every day. Didn't he realize what a big deal this was? Jonathan smiled to himself. No, of course he didn't. How could he?

"Hey, are you still there? Is that okay or not?" the man asked.

"Yeah, fine. Look, mail the money to this box number I'm gonna give you. Box number 3498. Maitland. Ed Maitland. Do you know how to spell that?"

"Yeah. It's right here on the piece."

"And it'll be in Thursday's paper?"

"Yeah, right, kid. Hey, your old man writes pretty well. He been at it long?"

"Yeah."

"Ask him to send anything else he's got. I could use more stuff like this. Gives the paper class. My readers get tired of bridal pictures and the minutes of the garden club."

"Yeah, thanks. Thank you very much!"

Jonathan hung up the phone, grabbed Liz into his arms, and swung her in circles. He kissed her cheek and they laughed wildly. As he explained everything, he made her promise not to tell a soul. It had to be his surprise.

With that, Jonathan was out the door to break the news to his father. He raced back to the cabin in his VW and charged into the cabin.

"Hey Dad!" he shouted as he entered the cabin. "Dad?"

He looked around. Maitland wasn't there.

Jonathan turned cold. Maybe he'd gone to town for booze.

"What a lousy time you picked to be out, Ed Maitland!" Jonathan shouted at the empty cabin. Then he hopped back into the VW and started for Stony River again.

It was late afternoon when Jonathan reached town a second time. His first stop was the bar. It was empty except for one man.

Then Jonathan checked the only other place that was open, the drugstore. Maitland wasn't there either.

"What's your trouble, Jonathan?" asked the tobacco chewer in front of the feed store.

"I can't find my dad," Jonathan replied.

The railroad cap beside the tobacco chewer chuckled. "How long he been gone?" he asked.

"Oh, just this afternoon."

The two old-timers exchanged knowing looks. "He in the habit of reporting his whereabouts to you, young fella?" The tobacco chewer slapped his thigh and burst out laughing at his friend's question.

"Look, I don't see anything funny in all this," Jonathan grumbled. "I've got something important to tell him. I'm worried, too. He must've gone on foot, and it's a cold, windy day to be going through the woods."

The railroad cap bit down on his pipe. "You call this cold? I 'member a day so cold you couldn't go from the drugstore to the hardware without freezing your ear lobes."

The tobacco chewer grunted. "That must've been '58 or '59. I 'member you'd spit and it'd freeze before it hit the ground."

"Look," Jonathan interrupted, "do you guys have any idea where my father might be?"

"Well, Ed's got a routine this time of year. He visits friends here and there. Some folks send out cards, but Ed visits," said the railroad cap.

"What friends?"

"Crazy Carl for one," the tobacco chewer said.

"Crazy Carl?" Jonathan repeated.

"Yeah. He lives out in an old bakery truck. Parks it in different places in the woods. Carl don't like to stay in one place too long for fear they'll catch him and tote him back to the hospital," said the tobacco chewer.

"Yep," agreed the railroad cap, "they'll take a snort together and talk about old times. Settle all the troubles of the world, those two will.

"You know," he continued, "Crazy

Carl's a real smart man. He can tell you the reason why World War I happened—and World War II. He knows all about how the world turned sour."

Jonathan realized that that was the extent of the information he could get in town. So he got in his VW and returned to the cabin, hoping to find Maitland home. But his father was nowhere to be found.

Jonathan tried to keep himself occupied by starting a fire. Yet he couldn't stop worrying.

He remembered what his mother had said, calling Maitland irresponsible. Right now, Jonathan couldn't agree more. He slammed his fist on the table and grumbled bitterly.

Then, through the woods, came the notes of *Silent Night* sung in an off-key voice. Maitland!

Jonathan hurried to the window. He saw Maitland ambling down the trail toward the cabin. He was no doubt drunk as a skunk, and he didn't give a hoot who knew it.

As he swung open the door, Maitland gave Jonathan one of his boyish grins.

"I suppose you're drunk, huh?" Jonathan fumed.

"Well, don't you sound like some old shrew waiting for her poor devil of a husband to come home!" Maitland slid a backpack off of his shoulders.

"You oughta be ashamed, worrying me like this. I didn't know what to think. It's dark and starting to snow!" Jonathan was so mad, he forgot his wonderful news.

"Listen, boy. I don't recall asking you to come here and worry about me."

"Yeah," Jonathan snapped, "you didn't even want to see your own son. Shows the kind of man you are!"

"I wouldn't have done you a favor, boy, if I *had* come to see you. Staying out of your life—now that was a favor. You didn't need some wine-soaked bum who couldn't succeed at anything hanging round your neck!

"You got a father, a good father. You got a good mother, too. You got all the advantages. You don't need me. You never needed me." Maitland's voice shook at the end.

Jonathan looked at the man and felt his eyes welling with tears. "Dad, the truth is, I did need you. And you needed me. I mean, nobody ever needed me before. You do. Don't you know what that means to me?"

Maitland blinked and cleared his throat.

"Where you been anyway?" Jonathan asked.

"Seeing a friend."

"Crazy Carl? Some people in town said you were a friend of his."

"Yeah. Carl's a mighty good man. They locked him up all those years 'cause they were scared of his smarts. He's invented a fuel that'll make oil obsolete, but they won't listen to him. The big boys just won't listen."

"You believe that?" Jonathan asked.

"I don't know," Maitland admitted. "Carl does. He's had a tough life. I figure somebody ought to at least act like they believe him. Can you understand that, Jonathan?"

"Yeah," Jonathan said. Suddenly Jonathan recalled what he'd been longing to tell his father all afternoon. "Hey, Dad, I've got some pretty neat news for you!"

Maitland stoked the fire. "Yeah?"

Now that he was about to give Maitland the news, Jonathan worried that his father might not be pleased. Not one bit. Maybe he'd hate Jonathan for meddling in his life.

Jonathan started out slowly. "Well, you see, I liked your articles and I knew other people would, too. So . . . well, I . . . I sent some of them to the *Courier*. And today, this editor, he called me back . . . Dad, one of your pieces will be in the paper for Christmas."

Maitland's hand went slack. He almost dropped the poker. His body froze and the color drained from his face.

Maitland quickly snapped out of his shocked daze and spun toward Jonathan. He grabbed the boy's shoulders and gave him a shake. "It's a joke, ain't it? A joke?"

"No, Dad, it isn't. I swear it isn't," Jonathan assured him, frightened.

"But it can't be," Maitland gasped. He let go of his son's shoulders and staggered back. "I sent them out, hundreds of times . . . till the paper turned yellow."

"I just picked out the three I liked best," Jonathan tried to explain in a calm voice. "This editor, he liked them a lot. They're going to pay you fifty dollars for each.

"And another thing: the editor wants more of them. He says your articles give his paper class."

Maitland stared. "It's all true? You ain't lying to me?"

"It's true."

Maitland sat down on the edge of his cot. He hung his head for a moment, then shook his head from side to side. "You mean, honest to God, my stuff is gonna be published?"

"Honest to God," Jonathan said, softly.

Maitland rose slowly. It was dark in the cabin, but Jonathan saw the tears streaming down his cheeks.

"Dad . . . "

Without a word, Maitland grabbed Jonathan and hugged him.

10 THE CHECK ARRIVED in the post office on Wednesday morning. Maitland looked at it for a long time. Then he let out a long, ear-piercing howl and rushed down Main Street.

Jonathan and his father went in every store to spread the news. People who saw them at first thought they were both drunk.

But Ed Maitland was the picture of sobriety. He was clean-shaven, his wild hair had been slicked straight down, and he wore his best lumber jacket.

"Heaven's sake, Ed, I never knew you were a writer!" Mr. Finch exclaimed, scratching his red hair. "Why, the *Courier* circulates all over the state!"

"What's your story about?" asked Mrs. Finch.

"About the wilderness," Jonathan put in. "Like Thoreau used to write."

"Ahhhhh, come on, Jonathan," Maitland protested. But he was obviously delighted by the comparison.

"A real writer, eh?" asked the railroad cap.

"You mean your name's really gonna be in the paper under an article?" asked the tobacco chewer.

"Why, I'll be darned," gasped the hardware store owner. "Nobody 'round here has ever even written a letter to the editor!"

* * *

On Christmas morning, Jonathan and his father came into town to get the paper. And there it was, Ed Maitland's story, along with a beautiful illustration of an antelope. Jonathan and his father read their copies in the VW.

"It's really neat," Jonathan said.

"Well, it's just a small article in a small-town paper but . . . "

"It's right there in black and white, and they paid you for it!" Jonathan said.

"Not much," said Maitland, but a smile dangling at the corner of his mouth soon swept over his whole face. He sucked in his breath and shouted, "Ed Maitland has been *published*!"

"All right!" Jonathan yelled, hitting the horn for all he was worth.

Before Jonathan left Stony River, he had a cup of coffee with his father in the cabin. Maitland stared into his cup awhile, then said, "Well, Jonathan, you've given me a lot. More than I had a right to."

"You've given me more," Jonathan said.

Maitland laughed.

"What I feel inside. What I feel about me . . . " Jonathan started. He couldn't find just the right words to describe it.

Finally he said, "I feel better inside than I've ever felt. I felt so cut up in Heritage Hills, like parts of me were missing."

Jonathan looked into his father's eyes. "I think I've finally found all of me."

"You better go. It'll be dark before you know it." Maitland's voice turned a little husky.

"I'll be coming back, Dad. I want to see if the yellow-rumped warbler really turns yellow as an egg yolk. And if he sings sweet as you say."

Maitland nodded, his lower lip trembling

a little. "When you come, I'll be sober, Jonathan. I swear."

They shook hands, found it wasn't enough, and then hugged the breath out of one another.

As Maitland walked Jonathan to the VW, Jonathan asked, "Will you tell Liz goodbye for me?"

Maitland smiled at his son. "Sure."

Jonathan grinned in return and hopped into the VW. "Tell her I'm coming back in a few months to take her dancing."

Jonathan started the motor and headed east for home. He knew he was leaving a part of himself behind in Stony River. And yet he was now whole in a way he'd never been before.